THE MUD FLAT MYSTERY

JAMES STEVENSON

Greenwillow Books · New York

For Jack

Watercolor paints and a black pen were used for the full-color art.
The text type is Novarese Medium.
Printed in Singapore by Tien Wah Press
First Edition 10 9 8 7 6 5 4 3 2 1

Library of Congress Cataloging-in-Publication Data

Stevenson, James (date)
The Mud Flat mystery / by James Stevenson.
p.   cm.
Summary: When a large box is delivered to Duncan while he
is away, the other inhabitants of Mud Flat are consumed with
curiosity about what might be inside.
ISBN 0-688-14965-0 (trade).   ISBN 0-688-14966-9 (lib. bdg.)
[1. Boxes—Fiction.   2. Curiosity—Fiction.]   PZ7.S84748Ms
1997   [E]—dc21   96-46269   CIP   AC

CONTENTS

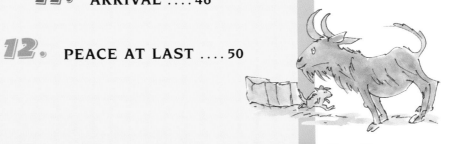

.1.
DELIVERY

It was a quiet morning in Mud Flat.
Gordon was digging in his vegetable garden.
Enid was watering her flowers, and Mark
was swinging gently in his hammock.

Suddenly, there was a strange sound:

"What in the world is that?" said Enid.

"It's getting nearer," said Gordon.

Hobart, the delivery man, came down the path.

He was wheeling a large cardboard box on his

squeaky handcart.

"That's a very big box, Hobart," said Gordon.

"Sure is," said Hobart.

"What's in it?" asked Enid.

"I don't open them," said Hobart. "I just
 deliver them."

"Where are you delivering it to?" said Mark.

"It's not for me, is it?"

"Or me?" said Enid.

"It's going to Duncan's house," said Hobart.

"Duncan is away on vacation," said Gordon.

"Then I'll leave it on his porch," said Hobart.

They all watched as Hobart went
down the path to Duncan's house
and pulled the handcart up the
steps. He left the box on the porch.

"That looked awfully heavy," said Enid
    as Hobart came back.
"Heavier than some," said Hobart.
"Not as heavy as others."
    He went up the path.

Gordon put down his trowel. Enid
stopped watering her flowers, and
Mark climbed out of his hammock.

They strolled down to Duncan's house.

·2·
WONDERING

By the time they reached Duncan's house,
there was already a small crowd standing
at the steps, staring at Duncan's box.

"I wonder what's in that box?" said Eugene.

"I wonder, too," said Albert.

"So do I," said Ruth.

"We'll find out when Duncan gets back," said Carl.

"What if Duncan has moved away without telling anybody?" said Ferdie. "Then the box will never get opened."

"In that case," said Norris, "maybe we should—"

"No, we shouldn't," interrupted Enid.

"For all we know," said Ralph, "Duncan could be on his way home this minute." Everybody turned around.

But there was no sign of Duncan.

.3.
EXPLORING

"You know what we need?" said Gordon.
"We need somebody who can crawl inside
the box, look around, and tell us what they
see."
"Estelle would be good," said Ralph.

"Where's Estelle?"

"Down here," said Estelle, "by your foot."

"Would you like to crawl into the box?" said Ferdie.

"Can't do it," said Estelle. "It's my nap time." She gave a tiny yawn.

"Just a quick tour?" said Ralph.

"All right," said Estelle.

Estelle wriggled up the steps of the porch.

When she reached the box, she found a small crack where the cardboard was folded. "Here I go," said Estelle, and she crawled inside.

"What's in there, Estelle?" called Grover.

"Darkness," said Estelle. "Very dark darkness."

"Is that all?" said Carl.

"Give me a little time," said Estelle.

Everyone was quiet.

At last Estelle wriggled out.

"What was it like, Estelle?" asked Enid.

"Some of it was round," said Estelle.

"Some of it was round," said Gordon to Janet.

"Some of it was flat," said Estelle.

"Some of it was flat," said Gordon to Janet.

"Some of it was thick, and some of it was thin," said Estelle.

"Thick and thin," said Gordon.

"Will you stop that?" said Janet. "I can hear perfectly well."

"Can you tell us what it was, Estelle?" said Carl.

"I don't know the name for it," said Estelle. She slithered off the porch and wriggled toward home.

.4.
SMELLING

"I'm worried," said Guthrie. "Whatever is in that box could go bad before Duncan gets back."

"How do you know it's food?" said Stuart.

"How do you know it's not?" said Guthrie.

"Why doesn't somebody go and smell it?" said Vicky.

"Good idea," said Stuart. "Who's the best smeller?"

"I'm an excellent smeller," said Gordon. He sniffed the air. "I can smell Naomi's cabbage soup all the way over by the mangrove swamp."

"I can smell that, too," said Guthrie.

"We can all smell that," said Stuart.

"You know what I can smell?"
said Janet. "I can smell the roses
in Dorothy's garden up on the hill."

"Everybody knows that Dorothy has roses,"
said Enid. "It doesn't mean you can smell
them from here."

"Let's not argue," said Carl. "I can smell
the garbage over at Guthrie's house."

"That's not garbage!" said Guthrie.
"I happen to be cooking a stew."

"My mistake," said Carl. "Sorry."

.5.
CHELSEA

Just then Chelsea came walking by.
"Here's Chelsea," said Stuart. "She's
the best smeller in Mud Flat."
"Why, thank you," said Chelsea.

"Would you mind going up on Duncan's porch and smelling that big box?" said Janet.

"I suppose I could," said Chelsea.

"That would be wonderful," said Guthrie.

"We'd all be very grateful."

Chelsea trotted up the steps.

She smelled the box.

She smelled the bottom
of the box.

She smelled all around
the box . . .

and up the sides.

Chelsea came down the steps.

"What did you smell, Chelsea?"
said Vicky.

"Tell us, Chelsea," said Guthrie.

"We all want to know," said Stuart.

"Cardboard," said Chelsea.

"*Cardboard*?" said Carl.

"Cardboard," said Chelsea.

·6·
GUARDING

By noon most people had left and gone
about their business.

But Ferdie and Norris were still there.

"You know what?" said Norris.
"Somebody might come
along and steal that box."
"Nobody from Mud Flat,"
said Ferdie.
"Of course not," said Norris. "A stranger."
"Two strangers," said Ferdie.
"Or one stranger with a handcart,"
said Norris.

"Somebody should guard that box,"
said Ferdie.
"That's right," said Norris, "but who?"

"Well, I could guard it in the daytime,"
said Ferdie, "and you could guard it
at night."

"I guard better in the daylight," said
Norris. "Much better."

"So do I," said Ferdie. "We can look
for a night guard later on."

Norris and Ferdie went up onto the
porch and stood on either side of
the box.

"My side is okay," said Ferdie.

"How's yours?"

"All quiet," said Norris.

.7.
DENT

Half an hour later Ferdie said,
"I wonder what we're guarding?"
"Me, too," said Norris.
"I don't want to be wasting my time
guarding nothing," said Ferdie. "Let's
give it a shake."

They tried to shake
the box. It hardly
moved.
"Harder," said
Ferdie.

The box began to tip.
"It's going to fall over!" said Norris. "Look out!"
They jumped away as the box toppled and
went tumbling down the stairs. It landed on
the ground with a clatter.

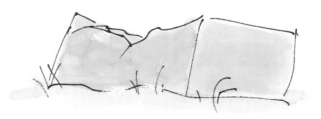

"Oh, my goodness," said Ferdie.

"Look at that big dent in the box,"
 said Norris.

"We've got to get that dent out before
Duncan gets home," said Ferdie.
"How?" said Norris.

"We'll open the box, I'll crawl in and
push the dent out," said Ferdie.
"Then I'll crawl out, and we'll glue
the box shut."
"How come you get to crawl in?"
said Norris. "I want to see what's
in there just as much as you do."

"I'm not going in to see what's in there,"
said Ferdie. "I'm going in to push the dent.
If I happen to see anything while I'm in
there, that's extra."

"Oh," said Norris. After a minute he said,
"I can push dents just as well as you can,
Ferdie."

"Okay, okay—we'll both go in," said Ferdie.
They tore open one end of the box.

Just then they heard somebody coming
down the path.

"Quick!" said Ferdie. "Get in the box!"

·8·
OLD
MR. WAFFLER

Old Mr. Waffler came shuffling down
the path.

As he passed the box, it moved a little.

"My goodness," said Mr. Waffler.

"Who's that?" called Norris.

"None of your business!" said Mr. Waffler,
and he hurried on down the path.

When he got to Janet's house, he said
to her, "You'll never believe what's up
the path."

"What is it?" said Janet.

"A monstrous box that moves and
speaks!" he said. "Run for your life!"

·9·
RESCUE

Janet went up the path to see what
Mr. Waffler could be talking about.
The box was thrashing around.

"Who's in there?" said Janet.

"It's me—Ferdie!" shouted Ferdie.

"And me—Norris! We're stuck!"

"Please get us out," called Ferdie.

"I don't know what to do," said Janet.

"Let me think."

 Along came Carl. "May I suggest
 getting Florence?" he said.

"Good idea," said Janet, and she left.

"Stay calm, boys," called Carl. "Help
 is on its way."

A few minutes later Janet came back with
Florence.

Janet said, "Norris and Ferdie are in the box,
and we thought perhaps you could help get
them out."

"I'll see what I can do," said Florence. She
backed up about ten feet. "Will everybody
please clear the way?" she said.

Everybody stepped to one side.

"Here we go," said Florence. She lowered
her horns and ran full tilt at the box.

Ferdie flew out of the far end of the box,
followed by Norris, followed by a shiny
new blue bicycle.

"Good work, Florence," said Janet.

"Are you okay?"

"I could be getting a slight headache,"
said Florence.

.10.
TESTING

"Nice bike!" said Mark.

"Beautiful!" said Estelle.

"Is it damaged?" asked Enid.

"I'll test it," said Ralph. He got onto the blue bike and went wobbling toward the woods.

"Do you really know
how to ride a bike,
Ralph?" called Carl.
"I'm learning," said Ralph.
"Does anybody happen
to know how to stop
a bike?"

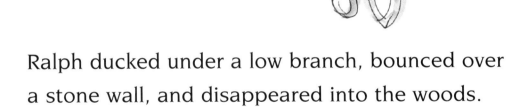

Ralph ducked under a low branch, bounced over
a stone wall, and disappeared into the woods.

"Good luck, Ralph!" called Grover.

"What about this box?" said Gordon.

"It's wrecked."

"Get it out of sight," said Estelle.

Ferdie and Norris dumped the box
behind Janet's house.

"Hi, everybody!" came a voice
from the path. "I'm back!"
"It's Duncan," said Guthrie.
"Oh-oh," said Ferdie.
"Oh-oh," said Norris.

.11.
ARRIVAL

"Did a box come for me?" asked Duncan.

"Box?" said Gordon.

"How big?" asked Norris.

"Big enough to hold a bicycle," said Duncan.

"Let me think," said Gordon.

At that moment Ralph came tearing
around the house on the blue bicycle.
He almost crashed into Duncan.
Ralph skidded to a stop.
"Welcome home, Duncan!" he said.

"Is that my new bicycle?" said Duncan.

"Why, it probably is," said Ralph. "We were
 all wondering about whose bicycle—"

"Never mind all that," said Duncan.

"Just give me my bike. I want to go
 for a ride."

Ralph handed it to him.

"I think you'll enjoy it, Duncan," said
 Ralph. "It rides awfully well."

But Duncan was already on his bike,
riding away.

"Whew," said Norris.

"From now on," said Ferdie, "we all
mind our own business."

Everybody nodded.

.12.
PEACE AT LAST

The next day Gordon went back to his gardening, and Enid watered her flowers, and Mark swung gently in his hammock.

"We had a lot of excitement yesterday,"
said Enid.

"We certainly did," said Mark.

"Peace at last," said Matthew.

Just then, they heard a noise:

SKA-REECH. SKA-REECH.

Hobart came down the path pushing
a big box on his handcart.

"Who's that for?" said Gordon.

HANDLE WITH CARE

SKA-REECH

"Andrew," said Hobart.

"Andrew's away, visiting his cousin,"
 said Enid.

"That's all right," said Hobart.

"I'll just leave it on his porch."
 He put the box on the porch
 and went away.

A few minutes later Duncan came
speeding by on his new bicycle.
He hit the brakes.
"What's that on Andrew's porch?"
he said.
"I don't know," said Ferdie, "and
I don't want to know."
"Me, either," said Ralph.
"Likewise," said Enid.

Duncan got off his bike. "I'm just a little curious, is all," he said.

He went up the steps. "Maybe I'll give this box a tiny shake." He shook the box gently. "I can't tell what's in here," he said.

"It's none of our business," said Mark.

Duncan shook the box harder, and it began to tilt toward him.

"Oh-oh," said Duncan. He stepped back and fell off the porch.

The box tumbled end-over-end
down the steps and landed
on Duncan with a thud.

"Hi, everybody!" called Andrew from down
the path. "I'm home!"
"It's Andrew!" said Ferdie.
"Did a big box come for me?" said Andrew.

Then he saw the box lying on the ground.
"That's my box!" he said. "What's it doing
there?"
"Is this your box?" said Duncan, peering
out from under it. "I had no idea."

"Here we go again," said Enid.